A New Friend for Hannah

by Elizabeth Dale and Sarah Lawrence

W
FRANKLIN WATTS
LONDON•SYDNEY

Chapter 1

"What a wonderful garden our new house has,"

said Mum. "Isn't it lovely and quiet?"

Hannah just sat on the swing and sighed.

Nothing felt right — it was too quiet.

At her old house, she and her friend, Suzy,

could call over the fence to each other.

She felt lonely at this new house.

Why did she have to move here?

"It'll soon feel like home," said Mum, giving

Hannah a hug. "Come on, let's unpack."

"In a minute," said Hannah.

Mum went inside and Hannah walked down the garden. Suddenly, she saw a beautiful rabbit hopping among the bushes. It was fluffy and the colour of toffee.

"Hello," whispered Hannah, holding out her hand.

The rabbit hopped over and sniffed her fingers.

His whiskers tickled! Hannah stroked him gently.

He was so soft and cuddly.

"I shall call you Toffee," she said. "You will be my friend forever."

They played hide and seek among the bushes. After a while, Toffee sat down. He looked a bit tired so Hannah carried him into the shed.

She fetched him some leaves and a blanket for a bed. Toffee looked happy, and so did Hannah.

7

Hannah went back to the house for lunch.

"You look happier," said Mum. "Do you like the garden?"

"Yes!" grinned Hannah.

She wanted to tell her mum about Toffee,
but she couldn't. Hannah was sure that Mum
wouldn't let her keep him.

Chapter 2

After lunch, Hannah went to get Toffee.

They played in the garden together.

Toffee hopped happily among the bushes.

"Barnaby! Barnaby!" called a girl from

the other side of the hedge. Hannah jumped at

the sound of the voice and Toffee's ears twitched.

"Maybe the girl is calling her brother,"

Hannah thought. She picked Toffee up

and hugged him.

"Barnaby!" the girl called again.

"Mum! I can't find Barnaby anywhere."

"Barnaby!" called a woman's voice. Toffee's ears

twitched again. He knew the sound of the voices.

Oh no! Hannah couldn't pretend any longer.

Toffee was really called Barnaby and he belonged

to the girl next door. Any minute now, the girl

might peer through the hedge and see him!

Quickly, Hannah picked up Toffee and hid behind the shed.

"That girl doesn't need a friend as much as I do, does she, Toffee?" Hannah whispered to him.

"I don't know anybody here except you."

The girl next door sounded really upset.

"What if Barnaby has hopped out on to the road?"

Hannah heard her sob. "What if he's been run over?"

"Don't worry, Mia. We'll find him, I'm sure,"

her mum said.

"But he always comes when I call!" Mia cried.

"Why isn't he coming?"

17

Chapter 3

As Toffee wriggled in her arms, Hannah started

to feel bad. The rabbit belonged to Mia. Hannah

couldn't keep him. She knew what she had to do.

She ran to the hedge, clutching Toffee.

"Have you lost a rabbit?" she called.

"I've found one!"

"Have you got Barnaby?" Mia called through the hedge. "Oh thank you! Can I come through?" Before Hannah could answer, Mia and her mum came through a gate in the hedge that Hannah hadn't noticed before.

"Oh, Barnaby!" Mia cried, gently taking him.

Hannah felt so sad.

She had lost her new friend already.

Hannah's mum came to see what was going on.
"Hello!" she said. "We've just moved in."
"Welcome!" said Mia's mum. "We came through
the gate in the hedge. I hope you don't mind?
We've always used it. Mia's best friend
used to live here."

"I miss her," said Mia, sadly.

"I miss my friends, too," said Hannah.

The girls looked at each other.

"Would Mia like to stay and play?"

asked Hannah's mum.

"Yes please!" cried Mia and Hannah together.

The girls had great fun playing with Barnaby.

As they played, Mia told Hannah all about her

school. "It's great there," she said. "You'll be in my

class. Our teacher is lovely."

Hannah smiled happily.

Chapter 4

"You were clever to find Barnaby," said Mum
as she tucked Hannah into bed that night.
Hannah frowned. She felt bad again.
"No I wasn't," she said. "I fed him and made a bed
for him in our shed. I hid him there so I could
keep him."

"Oh, Hannah, that was naughty!" said Mum.

"You must have known he belonged to someone."

"I did!" sniffed Hannah. "I'm sorry, but I was feeling really lonely, and he was my friend."

Mum looked at Hannah and smiled. "I don't think you'll be lonely here for long," she said.

Hannah smiled too.

She had made two great new friends today.

Maybe moving house wasn't so bad, after all!

Things to think about

1. Why does Hannah not like her new house at the start of the story?
2. Why do you think Hannah was happy to meet the rabbit?
3. What would you have done if you had heard Mia shouting over the hedge?
4. Do you think Mia is feeling a bit lonely, like Hannah was? What has happened to make her feel like that?

Write it yourself

One of the themes in this story is making friends. Can you write a story with a similar theme?

Plan your story before you begin to write it.
Start off with a story map:
• a beginning to introduce the characters and where your story is set (the setting);
• a problem which the main characters will need to fix;
• an ending where the problems are resolved.

Get writing! Try to use interesting adjectives, such as lonely, to describe your characters and make your readers understand them.

Notes for parents and carers

Independent reading

This series is designed to provide an opportunity for your child to read independently, for pleasure and enjoyment. These notes are written for you to help your child make the most of this book.

About the book

Hannah has just moved, and she is really missing her friend who lived next door to her old house. Then Hannah spots a pet rabbit in the garden. She is thrilled to have made a friend. But it is clear that the rabbit belongs to her new next door neighbours, and Hannah must make a decision.

Before reading

Ask your child why they have selected this book. Look at the title and blurb together. What do they think it will be about? Do they think they will like it?

During reading

Encourage your child to read independently. If they get stuck on a word, remind them that they can sound it out in syllable chunks. They can also read on in the sentence and think about what would make sense.

After reading

Support comprehension and help your child think about the messages in the book that go beyond the story, using the questions on the page opposite.
Give your child a chance to respond to the story, asking:
Did you enjoy the story and why?
Who was your favourite character?
What was your favourite part?
What did you expect to happen at the end?

Franklin Watts
First published in Great Britain in 2018
by The Watts Publishing Group

Series Editors: Jackie Hamley and Melanie Palmer
Series Advisors: Dr Sue Bodman and Glen Franklin
Series Designer: Peter Scoulding

A CIP catalogue record for this book is
available from the British Library.

ISBN 978 1 4451 6287 4 (hbk)
ISBN 978 1 4451 6289 8 (pbk)
ISBN 978 1 4451 6288 1 (library ebook)

Printed in China

Franklin Watts
An imprint of
Hachette Children's Group
Part of The Watts Publishing Group
Carmelite House
50 Victoria Embankment
London EC4Y 0DZ

An Hachette UK Company
www.hachette.co.uk

www.franklinwatts.co.uk